ADVENTURES OF
TOM THUMB

Retold by
David Cutts
Illustrated by
Fuka

Troll Associates

Library of Congress Cataloging in Publication Data

———

Adventures of Tom Thumb.

Summary: Relates a tiny boy's adventures in a
cow's mouth, a fish's belly, on the back of a mouse,
and at King Arthur's table.
   [1. Fairy tales. 2. Size—Folklore. 3. Folklore—
England] I. Jacobs, Joseph, 1854-1916. II. Hervert,
Fuka, ill. III. Tom Thumb. IV. Title.
PZ8.C96Ad   1988   398.2'1'0924   [E]   87-10980
ISBN 0-8167-1071-6 (lib. bdg.)
ISBN 0-8167-1072-4 (pbk.)

Copyright © 1988 by Troll Associates, Mahwah, N.J.

ADVENTURES OF
TOM THUMB

In the days of King Arthur, when people believed in magic, there lived a wonderful magician named Merlin. He could change himself into any shape and do almost anything he set his mind to. One day he happened to be traveling through the kingdom disguised as a beggar. Around supper time, he came to a cottage that belonged to a poor woodsman, so he knocked on the door and asked for something to eat.

The woodsman's wife gave him a thick slice of bread and some hot soup. Merlin noticed that the cottage was clean and bright, but for some reason the woodsman and his wife did not seem to be happy. Finally the magician asked them why they were so sad.

"I wish we had a child," sighed the woman. "Even if he was no larger than my husband's thumb, we would love him dearly." Merlin chuckled at the thought of such a tiny child. In fact, it pleased him so much that he decided to make the woman's wish come true.

A short time later, the woodsman's wife had a baby who was no bigger than her husband's thumb. The queen of the fairies came to visit the baby, for never had there been a child so small. She kissed him and named him Tom Thumb, because of his size. Then the other fairies set about making special clothes for him.

Tom never grew any bigger than his father's thumb. But he did grow up to be a clever fellow who was full of tricks. When he was old enough to go out and play marbles, Tom sometimes lost the ones he owned. Then he would creep into his friends' marble bags, stuff his pockets with their marbles, and return to the game. But one day he was caught in the act, and the other boy quickly pulled the string to close the top of the bag. Poor Tom was bounced around inside and was so badly bruised that he promised never to steal anything else as long as he lived.

A short time later, Tom's curiosity almost did him in.
His mother was making some pudding, and Tom wanted
to watch. So he climbed to the edge of the pot and leaned

over. But he leaned a bit too far and fell in! His mother
did not see him and stirred him around with the spoon.
Tom spluttered and squirmed so much that it looked as if
the pudding was bewitched. His mother took the pot of
pudding and threw it out the door.

Now as it happened, a beggar was passing by when the pudding came flying out the door. He picked it up and walked off with it. But by this time, Tom had gotten the pudding out of his mouth and was able to cry out at the top of his lungs. This frightened the beggar so much that he dropped the pot and ran for his life.

Tom wriggled free and walked home, covered with pudding. His mother gave him a kiss, washed him off in a cup of water, and tucked him into bed to rest.

Shortly after that, Tom's mother went out to milk the cow, and she brought Tom along. The wind was blowing briskly through the meadow, and Tom's mother was afraid he might be blown away. So she took out a piece of thread and tied him to a thistle. This was a fine idea, except that the cow happened to look down and see Tom's oak-leaf hat. In a single mouthful, the cow took up Tom and the thistle, and began to chew.

Tom scrambled about trying to keep away from the cow's teeth. "Mother! Mother!" he cried.

Tom's mother looked around to see what the trouble was, but of course she could not find Tom. "Where are you, Tommy?" she cried. And Tom wasted no time in telling her that he was inside the cow's mouth.

By this time, the cow had begun to wonder what was going on inside, so she opened her mouth and let Tom drop out. Tom's mother quickly held out her apron and caught Tom before he hit the ground. After that, she was a bit more careful where she took her tiny son.

One day a raven swooped down and picked Tom up, then flew off with him. When they were far out over the sea, the raven let Tom go, and he fell down into the ocean. That would have been the end of the boy, except that he was swallowed by a huge fish. The fish was caught a moment later and taken to the kitchen to be cooked for King Arthur's dinner. You can imagine the cook's astonishment when he opened up the fish and Tom jumped out!

Tom was brought directly to the king, for no one had
ever seen a boy as small as a man's thumb. He quickly
became a favorite in the court, where he amused the king
and queen and brought laughter to the Knights of the
Round Table.

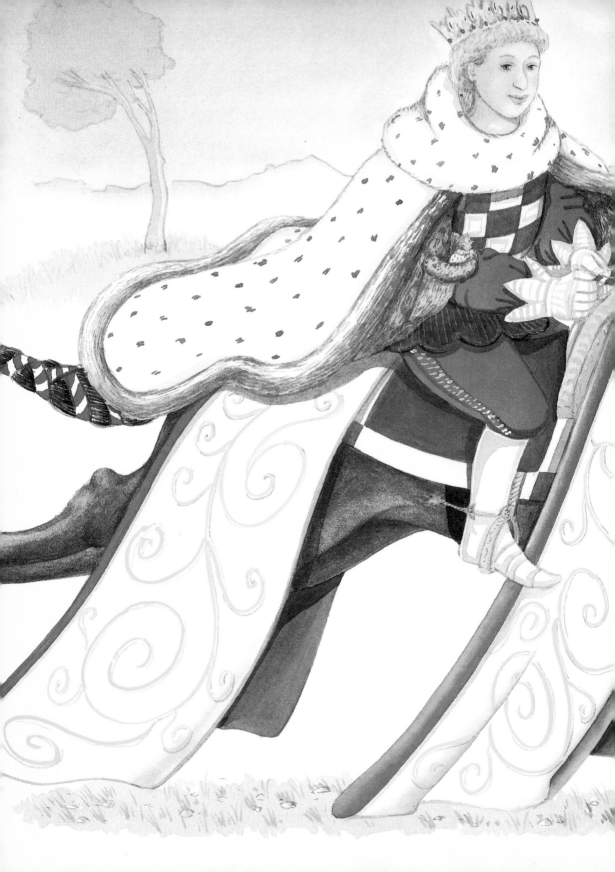

When King Arthur went riding on his horse, Tom often went along with him. Together they would ride through the countryside, visiting different parts of the kingdom. If they were away from the castle and it happened to rain, Tom crept into the king's pocket, where it was dry.

One day, King Arthur sent for Tom and asked about his family. He wanted to know if Tom's parents were the same size as Tom, and if they were wealthy or poor. Tom replied that his mother and father were the same size as any of the members of the king's court, and that they did not have much money at all. King Arthur immediately took Tom to the royal treasury, where he kept all his money.

"You may take as much home to your parents as you can carry," said the king.

Tom was delighted. He found a purse and put one gold coin in it. That was all he could carry. After a great many tries, he managed to get the purse up onto his back, but it was so heavy that he had to stop and rest four times every hour. He traveled for two full days before he finally reached his parents' home. He was so exhausted that his mother brought him inside and put him to bed. But the following day, Tom was back at the court.

King Arthur ordered a new suit of clothes to be made
for Tom. They were made out of butterfly wings and
were very dashing. Instead of a sword, Tom had a needle
hanging at his side. And instead of a horse, he rode on
the back of a mouse. Whenever he went hunting with the
king, Tom was a merry sight to see!

The king was so fond of Tom that he had a tiny
palace built for him. It was made out of gold, and the
doors were scarcely an inch wide. The furniture inside
was just the right size for Tom, who lived in the golden
palace quite comfortably. The king also gave him a tiny
coach that was drawn by six white mice. This made it
easy for Tom to visit his parents whenever he wished.

And so he lived a long and happy life, even though he
was no bigger than his father's thumb!